November 16, 2004

To: Sadie Jane
    I hope you enjoy this
Very special story.
                Cathy Helowicz

On

Grandpop's

Lap

Written by: Cathy Helowicz
Illustrated by: Ginger Doyel

Special Thanks:
To Donna, my sister-in-law and best friend. I cannot thank you enough for your help and support. Without your friendship and guidance, I don't know what I would do.

I would also like to thank everyone who has helped and supported me throughout this project.

On Grandpop's Lap

By Cathy Helowicz
Illustrations by Ginger Doyel

Published by Bodkin Pointe Press

For information or to place an order log onto the website: www.bodkinpointepress.com or send an email to: books@bodkinpointepress.com

First U.S. Edition, 2004

ISBN 0-9752684-0-6

Library of Congress Control Number 2004091843

Printed in Hong Kong

For my Dad

Grandpop loved his grandsons and Zachary was the oldest of two.

When Zachary would come to visit, he didn't know what to do.

He would run around in the house and get under Grandmom's feet.

Or bang on pots and pans, without any type of beat.

Grandmom would chase after Zachary with a mean look in her eyes.

Grandpop just shrugged his shoulders; it wasn't at all a surprise.

So Grandpop finally sat Zachary down to figure out what to do. Then gently pulled him onto his lap, to talk to him about a thing ... or two.

As Zachary sat on his Grandpop's lap, he looked up with his eyes so wide. Then he began to fidget, bouncing from side to side.

Grandpop looked down and said, "We need to keep you occupied."

"How about we read
a book, or go outside
and play?"

Zachary just shook his head, "No, I don't think
so, not today."

"Then we could play
a game or watch a
video... or even two."

"No, Grandpop that just won't do, I don't want to
watch a video, not even two."

Grandpop thought for a moment then said, "Okay, I've got it now! You could color some pictures; you could draw and color a cow."

Zachary thought for a moment before he
shook his head. "No, I don't think so Grandpop,
think of something else instead."

Grandpop sat there patiently trying to think of something to do. And Zachary sat there quietly, just waiting for him to choose.

All Zachary really wanted was to sit there on his lap, have Grandpop tell him a story or even just take a nap.

Zachary loved his Grandpop and just sitting there was enough. But he wanted to make Grandpop happy and would do any old stuff.

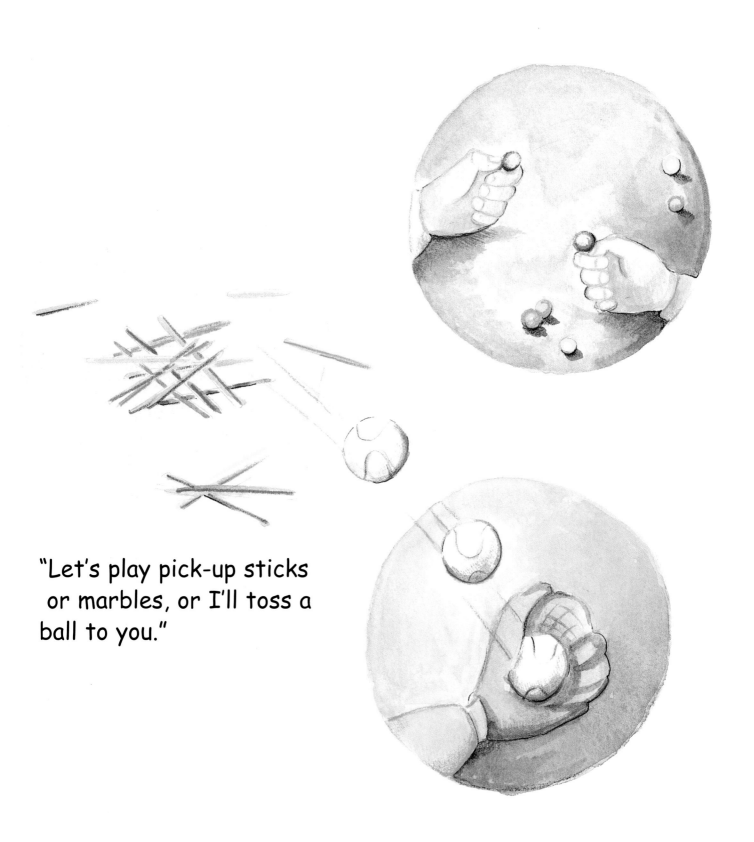

"Let's play pick-up sticks or marbles, or I'll toss a ball to you."

"No." Zachary timidly said, "But I know what we could do."

"How about we just sit here Grandpop? I'll sit here on your lap. You could tell me stories or just talk; how about that?"

Grandpop finally realized what Zachary wanted to do. He started telling him a story, one that was even true.

He laid his hand upon Zachary's head, "You are so
sweet and kind. I will tell you a story that will
occupy your mind."

Zachary was so happy; he was doing what he wanted to do. Just sitting on his Grandpop's lap and listening to a story... or even two.

"When I was a young boy I would occupy my mind. I would sit on my Grandpop's lap, sometimes for a very long time.

And my Grandpop would tell me stories about when
he was a little boy. Of the different games he played
or how he shared his toys."

Zachary sat there listening, looking into his
Grandpop's eyes. So full of love and admiration,
and even some surprise.

Wow, when Grandpop was little he was just like me.
Just wanting to sit on his Grandpop's lap, just
wanting to be.....

with his Grandpop.

zachary

Age 8½